LEVEL 5

Re-told by: Jocelyn Potter
Series Editor: Melanie Williams

Pearson Education Limited
Edinburgh Gate, Harlow,
Essex CM20 2JE, England
and Associated Companies throughout the world.

ISBN: 978-1-4082-8870-2

This edition first published by Pearson Education Ltd 2012

1 3 5 7 9 10 8 6 4 2

Set in 15/19pt OT Fiendstar
Printed in China
SWTC/01

Published by Pearson Education Ltd in association with
Penguin Books Ltd, both companies being subsidiaries of Pearson Plc

For a complete list of the titles available in the Penguin Kids series please go to www.penguinreaders.com.
Alternatively, write to your local Pearson Longman office or to: Penguin Readers Marketing Department,
Pearson Education, Edinburgh Gate, Harlow, Essex CM20 2JE, England.

"Stop, thief!" shouted Frollo, the Minister of Justice. He hated gypsies, and the woman had something in her arms. He rode faster.

The woman ran through the streets of Paris to the Cathedral of Notre Dame. The doors were closed. "Give us sanctuary!" she cried.

Suddenly, Frollo pulled the blanket from her arms. She fell and hit her head on the steps.

Frollo looked inside the blanket. "A baby!" he said. He looked at its ugly face. "A monster!"

Nobody could want a gypsy baby. Frollo decided to kill it.

But a priest ran from the cathedral. "Stop!" he cried. "Don't hurt the baby! You can't hide this from God."

Frollo looked up at the cathedral and felt afraid. "So what must I do?" he asked.

"The mother died," the priest answered sadly, "so you must bring up her baby."

"All right," Frollo agreed, "but the bell tower of your cathedral will be his home." Frollo named the baby Quasimodo.

Twenty years later, Quasimodo still lived in the bell tower.
Day after day, he rang the bells.

Quasimodo did not want to be a prisoner forever. There was a
festival in the square. He wanted to go. He told Frollo but Frollo
was angry.

"You can't go outside. You're an ugly monster," Frollo said.
"Out there, people will laugh at you. This is your sanctuary.
When your mother left you here, I brought you inside. I'm your
only friend."

Down on the street, Esmeralda, a beautiful gypsy girl, danced for money. A handsome captain named Phoebus watched her. When guards tried to take Esmeralda's money, Phoebus helped her escape.

"I'm your new captain," Phoebus told the guards. "Take me to the Palace of Justice."

Frollo welcomed him at the Palace of Justice. "I want you to stop those gypsy thieves," he told Phoebus. "They have a hiding-place somewhere in Paris. But today, they're at the festival. Let's go there."

Quasimodo *did* go to the festival. In the square people sang and danced, and some wore masks. They all watched when Esmeralda danced. Phoebus smiled. Frollo did not.

"Now," a man shouted, "we must find the King of Fools – the man with the ugliest face." He looked at Quasimodo. "And there he is! Is that a mask? No, it's his face!"

Quasimodo smiled happily. He was outside, and he was the king.

Suddenly, a guard threw a tomato which hit Quasimodo in the face. More tomatoes followed, and people laughed at the poor hunchback.

Quasimodo was unhappy and afraid. He tried to get away. He called to Frollo: "Master, please help me!"

Phoebus was unhappy, too. "Can I stop this?" he asked Frollo. "It's wrong."

But Frollo was very angry with Quasimodo. "Not yet," he said. "First, the boy must learn a lesson."

Esmeralda went to Quasimodo and cleaned his face. "Don't be afraid," she said kindly.

"Get away from him!" Frollo shouted.

"Why aren't you helping this poor man?" she cried. "You're the Minister of Justice, but there's no justice for him, or for my people."

"How can you speak to me in that way?" Frollo said. "You will pay for this!" He turned to Phoebus. "Captain, bring her here!"

Phoebus sent his guards to get her, but Esmeralda was too fast for them. She escaped again.

"I'm sorry, Master," Quasimodo told Frollo. "I'll never leave the cathedral again." He sadly went inside.

A few minutes later, Esmeralda ran into the cathedral, Phoebus followed her.

"Oh! Are you taking me to prison?" she asked him.

"I can't – the cathedral's a sanctuary," Phoebus answered.

"So what do you want?"

He smiled. "Your name. I'm Phoebus."

"I'm Esmeralda," she said softly.

Phoebus moved nearer, and …

"Good work, Captain!" Frollo called from the door. "Take her to prison!"

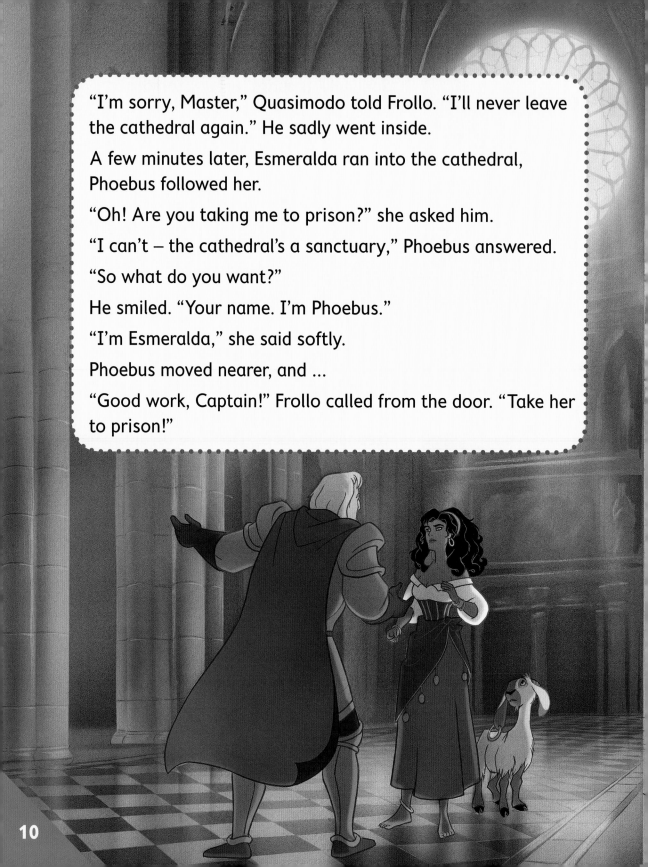

"I'm sorry, Minister. She has sanctuary here," Phoebus said.

"Then take her outside ..."

The priest arrived. "No!" he said. "Frollo, leave!"

Frollo walked away, but then he hid. When the priest led Phoebus out, Frollo caught Esmeralda's arm.

"This is a wonderful prison – but it's a prison," he said. Then, to Esmeralda's surprise, he smelled her hair. "I'll wait for you."

She pulled angrily away. "Why do you hate people who are different?" she cried. "Aren't we, too, children of God?"

Quasimodo listened and watched. Slowly, he moved down from the bell tower. But when he heard shouting, he ran upstairs again.

Esmeralda followed him to his room. "You have so much space up here!" she said.

"You're ... you're a wonderful dancer," Quasimodo said shyly. "Would you like to see my bells?"

"Yes, please."

So Quasimodo showed her the bells. Then he led her to the top of the building.

Quasimodo and Esmeralda looked out over Paris.

"You, too, can see this every day if you want to," said Quasimodo. "You have sanctuary."

"No," Esmeralda answered. "Gypsies can't live inside stone walls."

"But you're different from other gypsies. They're bad people." Quasimodo said. "My master told me."

"But Frollo is a terrible man."

"Oh, no," said Quasimodo. "He saved me. My family didn't want me because I'm a monster."

"You're *not* a monster," Esmeralda said. "Frollo's wrong about me – *and* about you."

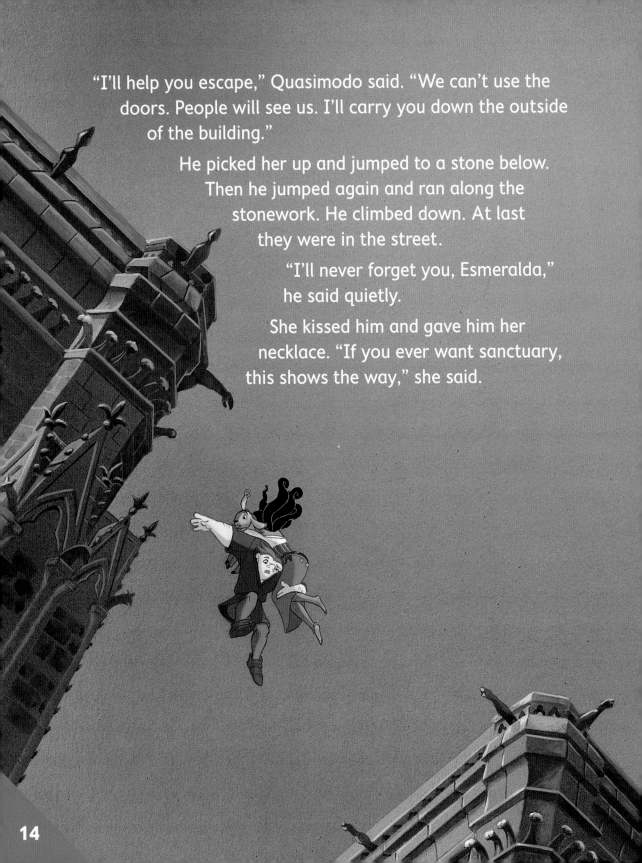

"I'll help you escape," Quasimodo said. "We can't use the doors. People will see us. I'll carry you down the outside of the building."

He picked her up and jumped to a stone below. Then he jumped again and ran along the stonework. He climbed down. At last they were in the street.

"I'll never forget you, Esmeralda," he said quietly.

She kissed him and gave him her necklace. "If you ever want sanctuary, this shows the way," she said.

When Quasimodo arrived back in the bell tower, Phoebus was there.

"No! This is a sanctuary. Go!" Quasimodo shouted at the Captain of the Guards.

"I don't want to hurt Esmeralda," Phoebus said. "I made her a prisoner here to save her life. Will you tell her that?"

"Yes, if you go now," Quasimodo said, and Phoebus left.

Quasimodo liked Esmeralda. She was beautiful and kind. "But I am ugly," he said.

Sadly, he rang the cathedral bells.

In the Palace of Justice, Frollo was afraid. "I'm a good man, better than other men," he said, "so why can't I get her out of my head? Her face, her hair, her eyes ... a fire is burning inside me. *She* did this to me! She must burn!"

A guard arrived. "Minister, the gypsy girl escaped from the cathedral," he said.

"I'll burn down every building," Frollo said, "and I'll find her. She must be mine – or she must die."

Frollo and his guards looked everywhere, but they could not find Esmeralda. Then they arrived at a poor house outside the city.

"We know nothing about any gypsies," the father of the family said.

"I don't believe you," Frollo said. He turned to Phoebus: "Burn the building, and the family!"

In the trees, Esmeralda watched and listened.

"No!" answered Phoebus angrily. "They aren't criminals!"

So Frollo burned the house. Phoebus ran inside and saved the children, and the parents escaped.

"For this, you will die!" Frollo shouted at Phoebus, and hit him.

Esmeralda jumped from the trees and frightened the guards' horses. Phoebus rode away on a horse, but he was hurt. He fell into the river.

"Leave him in there," Frollo told the guards when he arrived. "Now, find the girl! If you have to burn Paris to the ground, do it!"

After they left, Esmeralda ran quickly to the river. She jumped in and pulled Phoebus out.

Esmeralda brought Phoebus to the bell tower. Quasimodo was surprised, but happy, to see her.

"Will you help me again?" Esmeralda asked. "Phoebus is hurt and Frollo is looking for him. Can he stay here with you?"

"Yes," said Quasimodo sadly. He watched Esmeralda and Phoebus together and he saw their love. When they kissed, he cried.

Suddenly, he heard Frollo in the square below.

"You have to leave – now!" he told Esmeralda. He hid Phoebus under the table.

"You helped her escape!" Frollo shouted at Quasimodo. "I know that now. And Paris is burning because of you!"

"She was kind to me, Master," the hunchback said softly.

"She wasn't *kind*. She *used* you. Gypsies aren't kind. They can't feel love. Think of your mother!" Frollo stood quietly for a minute. "But all this will end tomorrow morning. I know the gypsies' hiding-place now. I will take my guards and I will kill them all!"

Angrily, he left.

Phoebus came out from under the table. "We have to get there first!" he said. "Are you coming?"

"I can't," Quasimodo said. "Frollo's my master."

"And Esmeralda's your friend," said Phoebus. "But where is she?"

Quasimodo thought. "The necklace!" he said, and he showed it to Phoebus. "It's a map of Paris. Look! Here's the cathedral, and here's the river. This little star shows the hiding-place."

They followed the map and found some stairs. The stairs led down, deep underground.

Quasimodo and Phoebus walked slowly below the city streets. Suddenly, the gypsies took them prisoner.

"These men are Frollo's friends!" said the gypsy king. "Kill them!"

"No!" shouted Esmeralda. "They're *our* friends. The Captain saved the family from the burning house. Quasimodo helped me escape from the cathedral."

"We came to tell you something," cried Phoebus. "Frollo's coming with his guards."

The gypsies started to run.

"Thank you." Esmeralda kissed Phoebus.

"Thank Quasimodo," Phoebus answered. "I followed *him*." Quasimodo smiled.

"*I* followed, too!" cried Frollo. He looked at Quasimodo. "For the first time, I could use you. You led me to this place."

Frollo turned to his guards. "Take the Captain and the gypsy girl away," he said. "There will be a fire in the square tomorrow for the girl."

"No!" cried Quasimodo. "Please, Master!"

Frollo looked at him angrily. "Take Quasimodo back to the bell tower," he told the guards. "Watch the building. This time, he must stay there."

23

The next day, the guards built a fire and put Esmeralda in the middle. Frollo stepped close to her.

"I can save you," he said quietly. "Choose me – or the fire!"

"The fire!" said Esmeralda angrily.

Quasimodo watched unhappily from above them. "*I* did this," he said. "Frollo wins."

But when Frollo started the fire, Quasimodo suddenly felt stronger. He jumped down from the cathedral and picked up Esmeralda. Then he carried her up to the bell tower.

"Sanctuary!" he cried.

"Take the cathedral!" Frollo cried to his guards.

Phoebus escaped from prison. "People of Paris, Frollo is burning our city. He's killing our people. Now he wants to take Notre Dame. Stop him!"

There was fighting in the square. Quasimodo dropped stones on the guards below, but some guards broke down the cathedral doors. Frollo climbed inside.

"What are you doing?" shouted a priest. "This is a house of God!"

But Frollo climbed up to the bell tower.

Esmeralda lay on the bed and did not move. Quasimodo watched and cried.

When Frollo arrived, Quasimodo said, "You killed her!"

"I had to, boy," Frollo said. "It hurts you, I know – but I can take that hurt away."

Frollo tried to kill Quasimodo, but the hunchback was stronger.

"The world *isn't* a terrible place," Quasimodo cried. "You told me that, but it isn't *true*. You are a terrible man!"

Suddenly, he heard a sound from the bed. Esmeralda!

Quasimodo picked her up and ran. Frollo followed quickly, and the two men fought on the outside of the tower.

"You want to save a gypsy?" Frollo cried. "Why am I surprised? Your gypsy mother died when she tried to save *you*."

What? His mother loved him! Quasimodo could not believe his ears.

"I made a mistake twenty years ago. I didn't kill you then, but I'm going to do it now," Frollo shouted.

And they fought again.

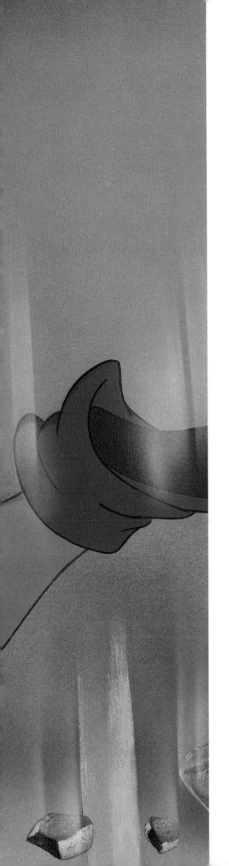

Frollo fell from the tower, but Quasimodo caught him. Then Quasimodo also fell, and Esmeralda caught his arm. She held him, but he was heavy. The people below watched, afraid.

Frollo found a stone with his hand and climbed on top of it. He smiled.

He could kill Esmeralda and Quasimodo, too.

Then the stone under Frollo's feet broke, and he fell down, down, down into the square below.

Esmeralda could not hold Quasimodo, and suddenly he fell, too. But two hands came out from a lower floor and Phoebus caught Quasimodo in his arms. He pulled him inside.

Esmeralda ran down to them. For the first time, the two men became friends. Esmeralda took Quasimodo in her arms, and then Quasimodo put her hand in Phoebus's. Theirs was the true love. He knew that now. *He* loved them in a different way. When they kissed, he smiled happily.

Hand in hand, Phoebus and Esmeralda walked out through the great cathedral doors. The people in the square laughed and clapped.

Then Esmeralda went inside again and took Quasimodo's hand. When Quasimodo stepped slowly, shyly out into the light, the people watched quietly. They were not sure about him.

A little girl went up the steps. She touched his face, and she kissed him. Then she led him down into the square. At last, the city welcomed the poor hunchback.

Activity page ①

Before You Read

① **These are the most important people in this story.**

  a Explain their jobs. Find new words in your dictionary.

Quasimodo,
bell ringer

Esmeralda,
gypsy dancer

Frollo, Minister
of Justice

Phoebus, Captain
of the Guards

  b Which of these jobs would you like? Why?
  Which would you not like?

  c Talk about the four faces. Which people look:

  happy?   kind?   handsome/beautiful?   old?
  unhappy?   angry?   ugly?   young?

② **This story begins more than five hundred years ago in Paris. The Cathedral of Notre Dame was a sanctuary for people who wanted to hide. What kind of people hid in the cathedral, do you think? Why?**

Activity page ❷

After You Read

❶ How did the person on the left save, or help, the person on the right?

ⓐ   ⓑ   ⓒ

❷ Finish the story with the right words.

> happy   kind   laughed   rang   Phoebus   Frollo
> gyspy   hunchback   cathedral   people

Quasimodo's mother was a ᵃ..... . After she died, he lived in the ᵇ..... . He ᶜ..... the bells. When, one day, he left Notre Dame, people ᵈ..... at him. Only Esmeralda was ᵉ.... to him. Later, Quasimodo helped her escape from ᶠ..... . He loved her, but she loved ᵍ..... . In the end, Quasimodo was ʰ.... for her – and the ⁱ..... of Paris learned to love the poor ʲ..... .

❸ What do you think?

a Why did some people in the story hate gypsies and hunchbacks?

b Do people feel different now about gypsies and hunchbacks? Why (not)?

c Are there people in your country who most people do not like? Who? Why? Is this right?